ISBN 1 85854 553 6
This edition produced by Brimax Books for
Index Direct Book Supplies, Kettering, NN16 8TD 1996.
Printed in Spain.

Christmas Storybook

Written by Alan Aburrow-Newman
Illustrated by Carole Gray

INDEX

The
Snowball
Express

Two piles of presents with rabbits' feet came walking along the snow-covered path. Jake and Billy were taking their gifts to Grandpa Root. Being careful not to drop their brightly wrapped presents, the two small rabbits followed the path to the edge of the forest.
The last tree they passed was an apple tree and hanging high on a bare branch was a single red apple.

"Oh Jake, look up there!" said Billy. "Hold my presents for me. I must climb up and pick that apple." "All right, but hurry," said Jake. Billy piled his presents on top of Jake's and started climbing the tree. Jake saw a log which looked like a good place to sit. As he walked towards it he tripped and fell head over heels in the snow and rolled down the hillside. After one roll, Jake was covered in snow. After two rolls he was a snowball.

The snowball, with Jake and the presents hidden inside, rolled down the hill until it eventually slowed down and stopped in a patch of deep snow.

Back at the top of the hill, Billy jumped down from the apple tree and looked around for Jake.

"Well, that's strange," he muttered as he munched on the apple. "Jake has run off with all the presents. I will have to catch up with him."

Using two strong sticks as poles, Billy skied down the hillside on his big, flat feet. "It is not all hard work when you are a rabbit," he laughed.

When he was halfway down the hill, Billy found the giant snowball. "This is a good place to take a look," he said, and climbed on top and looked down the hill. "I cannot see Jake anywhere. I wonder where he is?"

As Billy skied down the hill towards Grandpa Root's house, he heard a rumbling noise behind him. The giant snowball had started to roll and was chasing him. It was getting bigger and bigger.

"Oh, I wish Jake was here to help me," puffed Billy.

The snowball caught up with him. And after two rolls only his ears were sticking out. Then it knocked down a Christmas tree and a holly bush, and they disappeared inside too!

Grandpa Root was warming his toes by the fire when he heard the rumbling noise outside.
"I am expecting Jake and Billy with my Christmas presents," he said.
"But that does not sound like them."
Opening his door, he looked outside and saw the giant snowball charging down his garden path.

With a loud, wet thud, the giant snowball crashed against Grandpa Root's house and burst open. In a blizzard of snow, out flew Jake, Billy, all of the presents, the Christmas tree and the holly bush!

Jake and Billy sat in the snow surrounded by presents. The Christmas tree landed in the garden and the holly bush ended up hanging above Grandpa Root's front door.

"Oh, here you both are," said Grandpa Root, brushing the snow out of his eyes. "I was wondering where you were. I did not expect you to arrive by snowball!"

"Jake! Where did you come from?"
asked Billy, as he shook snow from
his ears.

"I was inside a snowball," said Jake,
dizzily. "Where did you come from?"

"I was looking for you and I was
eaten by a snowball, too," said Billy.
They both burst out laughing. "A
special delivery for Grandpa Root,"
laughed Jake.

"By snowball express," added Billy.

Can you find five differences between these two pictures?

Can you say these words and tell the story by yourself?

apple

presents

snowball

Christmas tree

Lester's Christmas Wishes

In the middle of the night on Christmas Eve, Lester the teddy bear was wishing for things. "I wish I had a bigger piece of Christmas cake than this," he grumbled. "I wish I had all those toys," he said, looking at all the presents under the Christmas tree. "And I wish my toybox was decorated like this room," he muttered, looking around at the beautiful garlands and streamers.

Fizz, the Christmas fairy, looked down at Lester from the top of the tree. "Stop grumbling, Lester," she said. "You have a lovely toybox, and you are lucky to have a piece of Christmas cake."

"But I wish I had more," said Lester, tugging at a chocolate on the tree.

As the tree shook, Fizz dropped her wishing star and Lester picked it up. "Great, I can wish for anything I want now," he said.

"Please be careful," said Fizz. "It takes a lot of practice to make good wishes."

"Easy peasy, watch this," said Lester, tapping the cake with the wishing star. "I wish I had a huge cake." There was a loud splodge and the room was filled with cake, which squashed Lester against the wall.

"Now what are you going to do?" asked Fizz.

Lester prodded the cake with the wishing star. "I wish this cake was smaller," he said.

The cake shrunk to the size of a plate.

"You could say that was as easy as pie...or cake," laughed Lester. Then he noticed the cream and cherries stuck all over the walls.

"What a mess!" said Fizz.

Lester tapped the wall with the star. "I wish there was nothing on these walls," he said. In a second there was not anything on the walls - not even wallpaper or paint!
"Well!" said Fizz. "I must say this looks very cheerful for Christmas."
"Oh, please help me," pleaded Lester. "I will give you back the wishing star if I can reach that high."

Before Fizz could warn him, Lester tapped himself on the shoulder with the star. "I wish I was as tall as a tree," he said. He started to grow...and grow...and grow until he filled the room! The furniture was broken and the Christmas tree was pushed into the corner.
"Oh no! Another mess up!" snapped Lester. "I wish I was small again."

"I will have to climb up to you," Lester called to Fizz.

"Be careful then," she said.

"Easy peasy," said Lester. He started to climb up through the branches. "Ouch!" he cried. "These Christmas trees are prickly!" Half way up, a particularly sharp jab made Lester forget how to climb trees and he found himself dangling from the end of a branch. The tree began to fall. "Help me!" shouted Lester as the tree gathered speed.

The tree swept the decorations from the ceiling and then crashed in a heap of tinsel, baubles and twisted branches. Lester and Fizz crawled out from underneath.

"This will be quite a nice surprise for Freddie when he comes down in the morning," said Fizz, brushing down her gown. "Just because you were ungrateful. Easy peasy indeed!"

"I am sorry, Fizz," said Lester, looking at the mess. "I have wished away everyone's Christmas."

"I will give you one last wish," said Fizz, "but it must be a very good one."

Lester thought about wishing for nice things to eat or play with; but he also thought how nice it would be to have Christmas back. So he made his wish. Fizz flew around the room with the wishing star and in a flash of light and a tinkle of bells it was beautiful again.

"Thank you," said Lester. "That was a good wish!"

Can you find five differences between these two pictures?

Can you say these words and tell the story by yourself?

Lester

Fizz

wishing star

cake

The
Magic Antlers

It was Christmas Eve. The floor of Santa's workshop was covered with scraps of string and Christmas wrapping paper. Sleepy elves and pixies yawned and dozed in armchairs around the warm fire. Pip, Santa's newest helper, was too excited to sleep. He looked up at the list of jobs that Santa had written on the board.
1) Make toys. 2) Wrap toys. 3) Load sleigh. 4) Get Reindeer ready.
5) Yawn and doze in armchairs.

53

"Oh no!" said Pip, running around in circles. "The reindeer are not ready. Wake up! Wake up!" he cried. "You have not done number four and Santa must leave soon."
Pip ran from elf to pixie, shaking and prodding, pulling ears and tweaking noses, but everyone was fast asleep and no one stirred. "Oh well," he said. "I will just have to help the reindeer myself."

Pip hurried to the reindeer's stable.
"Hello, I am Pip," said Pip. "All of the
other helpers are asleep so I have
come to help you on my own. Who
are you?"
"I am Dasher. Have you brought our
magic antlers?"
"Magic antlers!" gasped Pip.
"Why do you need magic antlers?"
"That is how we fly," said Dancer.
"They are in the secret room at the
top of the stairs. Go quickly!"

Pip rushed to get the magic antlers. He found them in the secret room at the top of the stairs. They were hanging from the wall.
Each magic antler had a name hanging from a golden loop. Dasher, Dancer, Prancer, Vixen, Comet, Cupid, Donner, Blitzen.

Pip knew he had to hurry. He carefully took all the magic antlers from the wall and went back down the stairs. But halfway down he tripped on his bootlace and tumbled into a heap at the bottom of the stairs.

The magic antlers landed in a tangle beside him. All the name tags had come off and were scattered across the floor.

"Now we are in trouble," said Vixen.
"You have mixed them up."
"Does it matter?" asked Pip.
"Yes," said Prancer. "Wrong antlers
feel strange."
"And they do funny things,"
said Cupid seriously.
"We can only fly properly with
our own antlers," said Comet.
"I am sure I can remember which
ones you should have," said Pip
hopefully. "Maybe you should try
them out."

63

Prancer took off but flew upside-down. Dancer got dizzy flying in circles. Vixen tumbled head over heels along the ground, and Comet got stuck in the Christmas tree.

"Oh, what a mess!" said Pip.

"A mess!" roared Blitzen. "It is a disaster. How can we pull Santa's sleigh when we are flying here and there all over the sky?"

"It was not my fault all the other helpers went to sleep," sobbed poor Pip. Tears dripped down his face and made puddles on the floor.

"Now, now," said Cupid softly. "We know you were only trying to help. It will not take long for us to find the right antlers, then you can have a ride in the sleigh."
Pip looked tearfully out from under his hat. "A ride in the sleigh?"

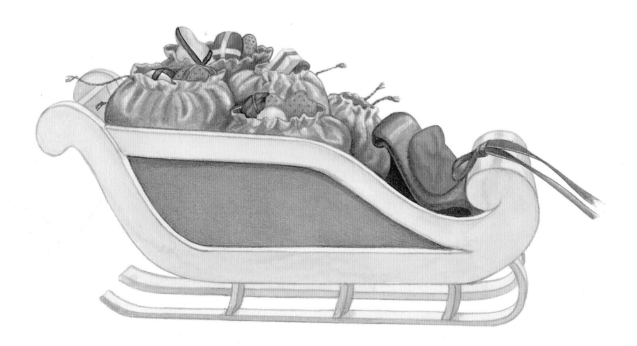

The reindeer swapped antlers and at last they could all fly properly. Just then, Santa rushed into the stable. "Quickly, quickly," he puffed. "We are late. You will have to fly like eagles tonight."
Tucked up warm and snug in the back of the sleigh, Pip could hear Santa as he whistled and called to the reindeer.
"Magic antlers!" he sighed happily as they passed in front of the moon. "That is how they fly!"

Can you find five differences between these two pictures?

Can you say these words and tell the story by yourself?

gifts

magic antlers

Santa

sleigh

Duffy's Christmas Message

Duffy the Squirrel was walking home through the town after visiting some friends when the Christmas lights were turned on. The main street looked wonderful. A huge banner with the message "Welcome Santa - Merry Christmas!" hung from the Town Hall on one side of the street to the library on the other. The little squirrel had never seen such decorations. Santa had never been to the forest where Duffy lived. The lights gave Duffy an idea. He would make a message for Santa.

Back in the forest, Duffy explained his idea to Sticky the spider. Then Sticky, together with his brothers and sisters, spun miles of silken thread. Small birds gently carried the spiders from tree to tree. The spiders looped the silk from twig to twig until the biggest spider web ever seen in the forest stretched across the clearing.

Duffy climbed to the top of the highest tree and looked down at the spider web sparkling under the evening frost. The spiders had spun a special message into the silken web. It read "Welcome Santa - Merry Christmas!"

"Wonderful," said Duffy. "Santa will see this from miles away."

Later, when the forest was in darkness, Duffy was woken by shouting from the clearing.
"Help me! I am stuck, get me out of this!"
Duffy hurried to the clearing at the same time as Sticky, who had also heard the yelling and shouting. Just as they arrived the moon came out from behind a cloud and lit up the clearing. Duffy was horrified.
Wizard, the old owl, was caught in the spider web.

"Duffy! Sticky! Come here!" roared Wizard. "I was quietly gliding along looking for some supper when suddenly I am stuck in a spider web big enough to catch a flying elephant. What are you up to?"

"Do not blame Sticky," said Duffy, stepping forward. "I made him help me. I wanted a Christmas present."

"Well you have got me," grumbled Wizard. "Am I what you wanted?"

"Not really," said Duffy. "I wanted some winter socks and a woolly hat."

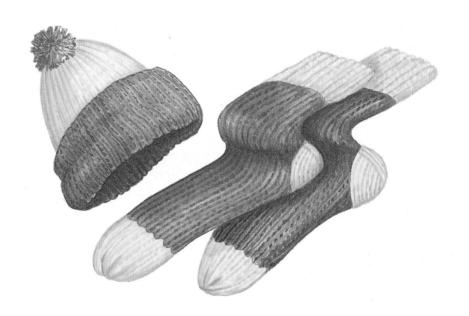

Sticky and Duffy untangled Wizard.
Still covered in silk threads, he sat
on a tree stump and glared at
Duffy. "Did you really expect a pair
of winter socks and a woolly hat
to be flying through the forest
on Christmas Eve?" he asked.
"Of course not," said Duffy.
"Then why did you set a trap?"
asked Wizard.
"I didn't," said Duffy. "It was a
message for Santa. It said 'Merry
Christmas' until you tangled it up."

Duffy started to cry. "Now Santa will not come to the forest with gifts for everyone," he sobbed.

Wizard put his wing around Duffy's shoulder. "I will take your message to Santa," he said kindly.

"Do you know where he is?" Duffy asked.

"Yes, of course," said Wizard. "Because owls and bluebirds are Santa's messengers. We tell him who has been good or naughty and we deliver the letters to him."

So Duffy wrote a letter to Santa. He said sorry for trapping Wizard and asked for some winter socks and a woolly hat. Then doing as he was told, he tied the letter with a red ribbon and hung it from the bush outside his house. All through the forest, the other animals did the same.

When they were sleeping, Wizard and hundreds of bluebirds flew silently away with the letters.

On Christmas morning, a delighted Duffy woke to find that Santa had been to the forest. Hanging from every bush and tree were small gifts. Hanging from Duffy's bush were winter socks and a woolly hat!

Can you find five differences between these two pictures?

Can you say these words and tell the story by yourself?

spider web

Wizard

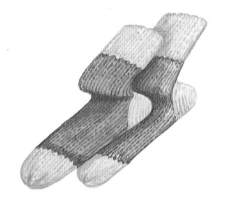

winter socks

woolly hat

93